Trucks Roll!

Trucks Roll!

WORDS BY George Ella Lyon

ART BY Craig Frazier

SIMON AND SCHUSTER
London New York Sydney

SIMON AND SCHUSTER

First published in Great Britain in 2007 by Simon & Schuster UK Ltd

Africa House, 64-78 Kingsway, London WC2B 6AH

A CBS company

Originally published in 2007 by Atheneum Books for Young Readers,

an imprint of Simon & Schuster Children's Publishing Division, New York

Book and cover design by Craig Frazier

The text for this book is set in Serifa.

The illustrations for this book are rendered by hand and digitally coloured.

A CIP catalogue record for this book is available from the British Library

ISBN -13: 978-1-84738-125-5

Printed in China

10 9 8 7 6 5 4 3 2 1

Trucks Roll!

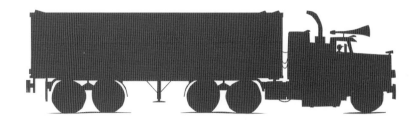

Trucks' wheels
go 'round and 'round.
Trucks' pistons
go up and down.

Trucks roll!

Trucks have trailers.
Trucks have cabs.
Some haul rabbits.
Some haul labs.

Some haul apple juice.
Some haul trees.
Water them down
in the desert, please.

Trucks roll!

Trucks bring ice cream.
Trucks bring blocks,
books and bulldozers,
dolls and clocks.

Dispatcher calls,
says Get underway!
Chocolate chip cookies
have to travel today.

Stacks of puzzles
ready to load.
Spaceships, toy trains –
get them on the road!

Haul them through mountains,
over rivers, past towns –
around blue sky curves,
through rain pouring down.

Trucks roll!

Steering wheel, radio,
horn's deep beep.
TV in the bunk
where tired truckers sleep.

Trucks stop.

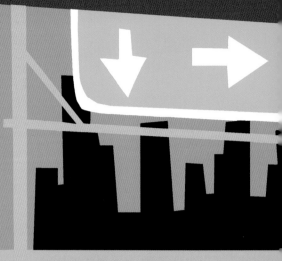

Stop for traffic lights.
Stop for tolls.
Stop for doughnuts
and bacon rolls.

Stop for services.
Stop for gas.
Stop for the night
to let sleepiness pass.

Stars above like headlight beams:
truckers travel rolling dreams.

Then, key in the slot,
coffee in the cup,
trucker's at the wheel
when the sun comes up.